A Tribute from Eric Carle

Happy 50th birthday, dear Swimmy.

Like all of Leo Lionni's work, *Swimmy* is a magnificent blend of story and graphics. Here, I feel, he has been more daring than ever. Both childlike and sophisticated, the images in the underwater environment glide by like a film across the screen. The jellyfish halfway through the book is similar to a potato print done by a kindergartner and is as sophisticated as the best art of our time. And this is true of all his creatures, big and small. I was especially intrigued by the forest of seaweed growing from sugar-candy rocks. Both words and pictures blend harmoniously. (Sugar-candy rocks! The Beatles would have loved that.) Lionni, ever inventive, using the ornamental edge on a napkin or doily, painted on it and made prints. The joy that Lionni must have felt while doing this couldn't possibly escape the viewer.

The story is as old as an Aesopian lesson of outwitting a bully. Here the big bad tuna fish not only intimidates and scares a peaceful school of little fish but— *horrors!*—gobbles them up. But don't worry, help is on the way. And charmingly, wittily, and most satisfyingly at that.

Recently I was asked whose picture books I could not live without. Guess my answer? You are right.

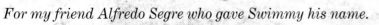

For my friend Alfredo Segre who gave Swimmy his name.

Swimmy

by Leo Lionni

Alfred A. Knopf, New York

A happy school of little fish lived in a corner of the sea somewhere.
They were all red. Only one of them was as black as a mussel shell.
He swam faster than his brothers and sisters. His name was Swimmy.

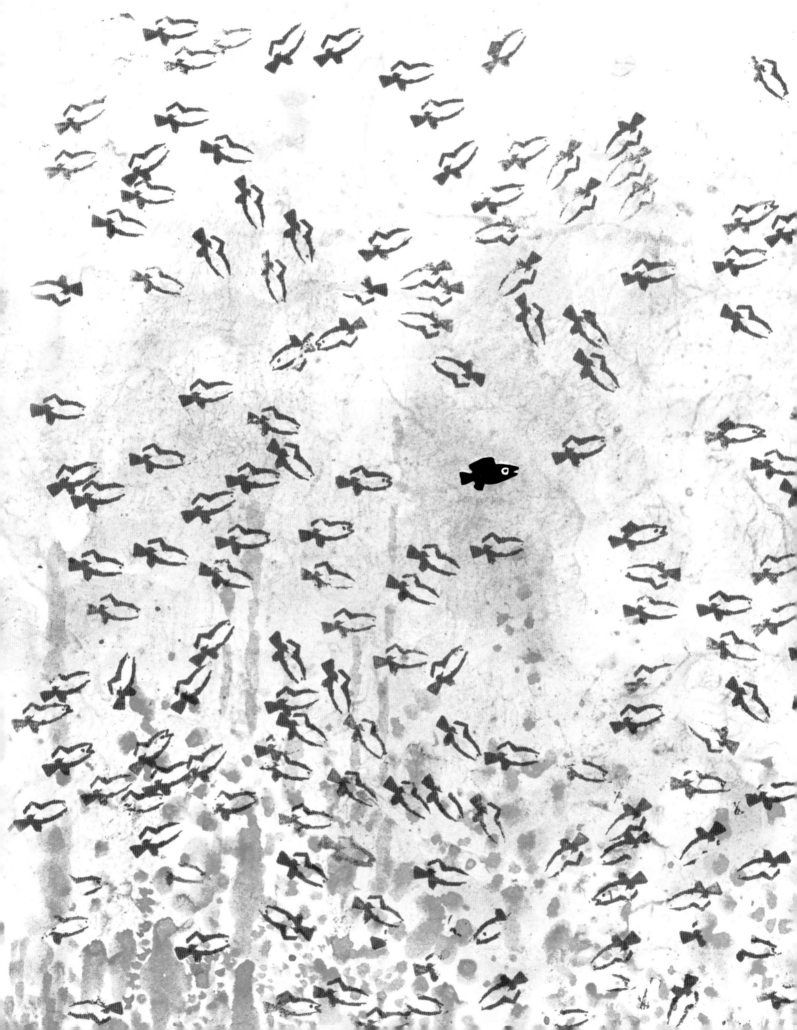

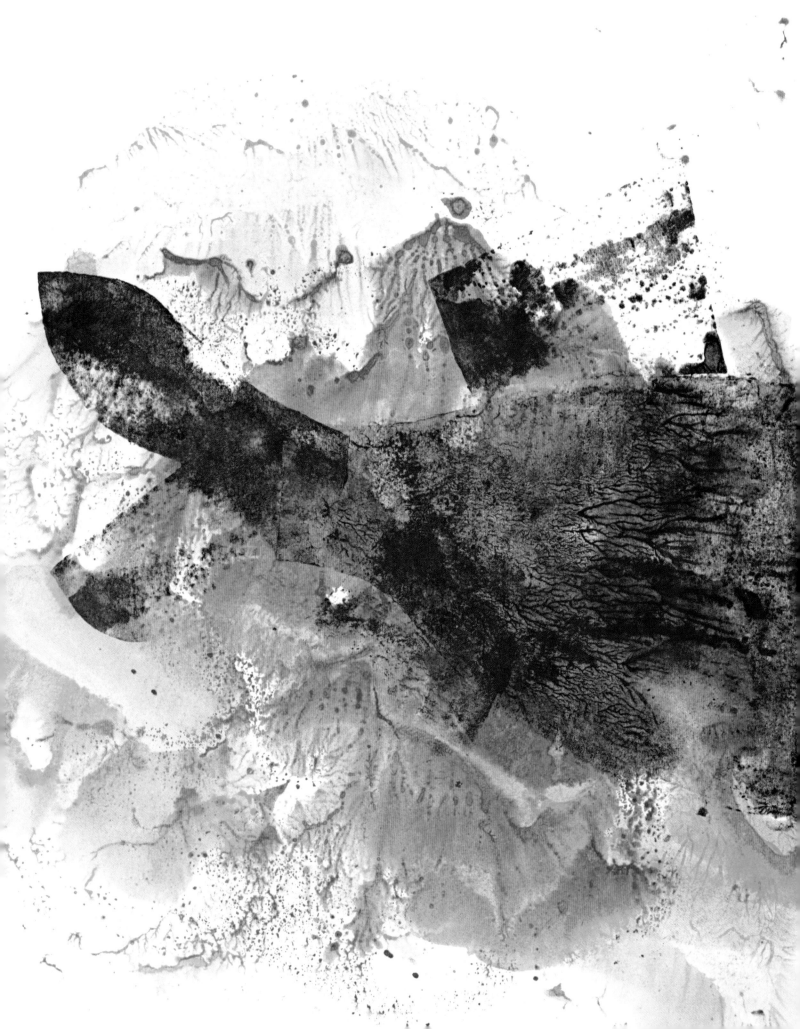

One bad day a tuna fish, swift, fierce and very hungry, came darting through the waves. In one gulp he swallowed all the little red fish. Only Swimmy escaped.

He swam away in the deep wet world. He was scared, lonely and very sad.

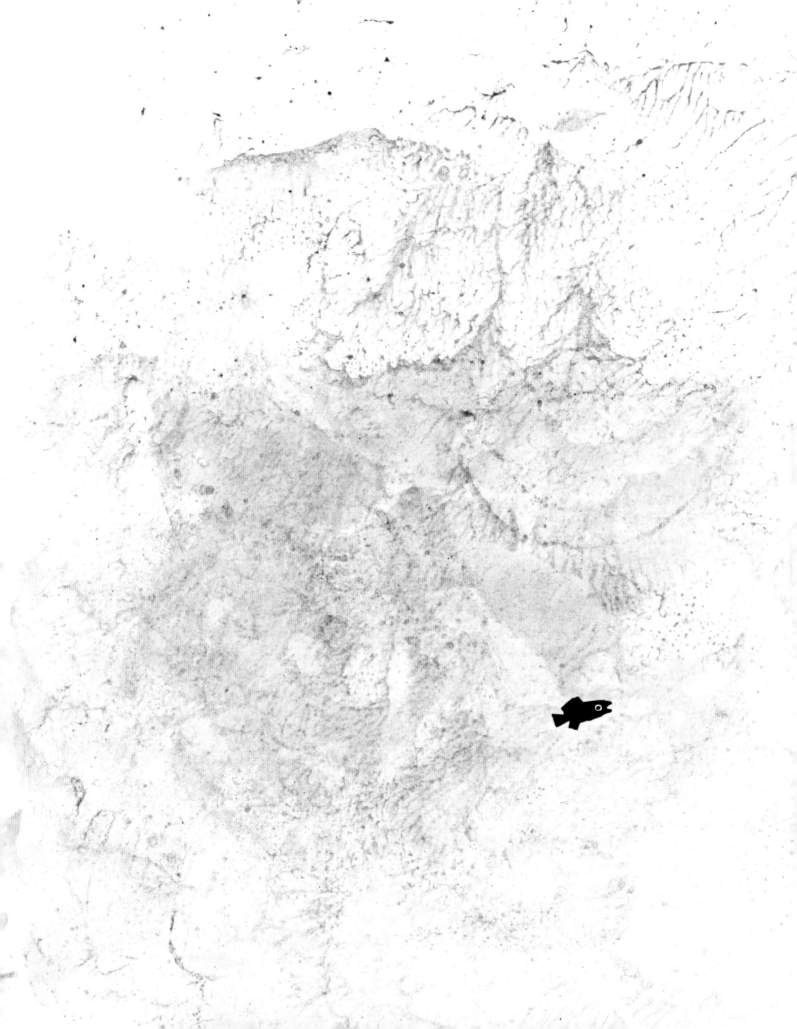

But the sea was full of wonderful creatures, and as he swam from marvel to marvel Swimmy was happy again.

He saw a medusa made of rainbow jelly . . .

A lobster, who walked about like a water-moving machine . . .

strange fish, pulled by an invisible thread . . .

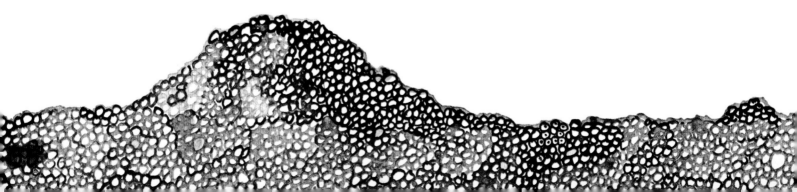

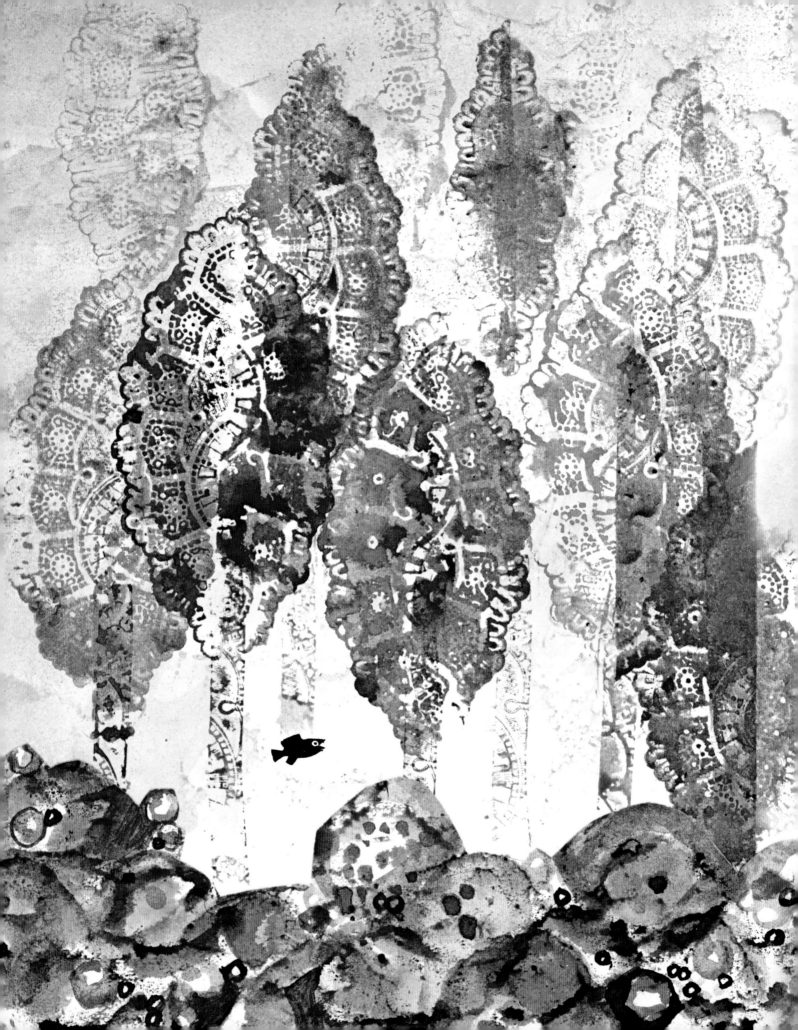

a forest of seaweeds growing from sugar-candy rocks . . .

an eel whose tail was almost too far away to remember . . .

and sea anemones, who looked like pink palm trees swaying in the wind.

Then, hidden in the dark shade of rocks and weeds, he saw a school of little fish, just like his own.

"Let's go and swim and play and SEE things!" he said happily.
"We can't," said the little red fish. "The big fish will eat us all."

"But you can't just lie there," said Swimmy. "We must THINK of something."

Swimmy thought and thought and thought.

Then suddenly he said, "I have it!"
"We are going to swim all together like the biggest fish in the sea!"

He taught them to swim close together, each in his own place,

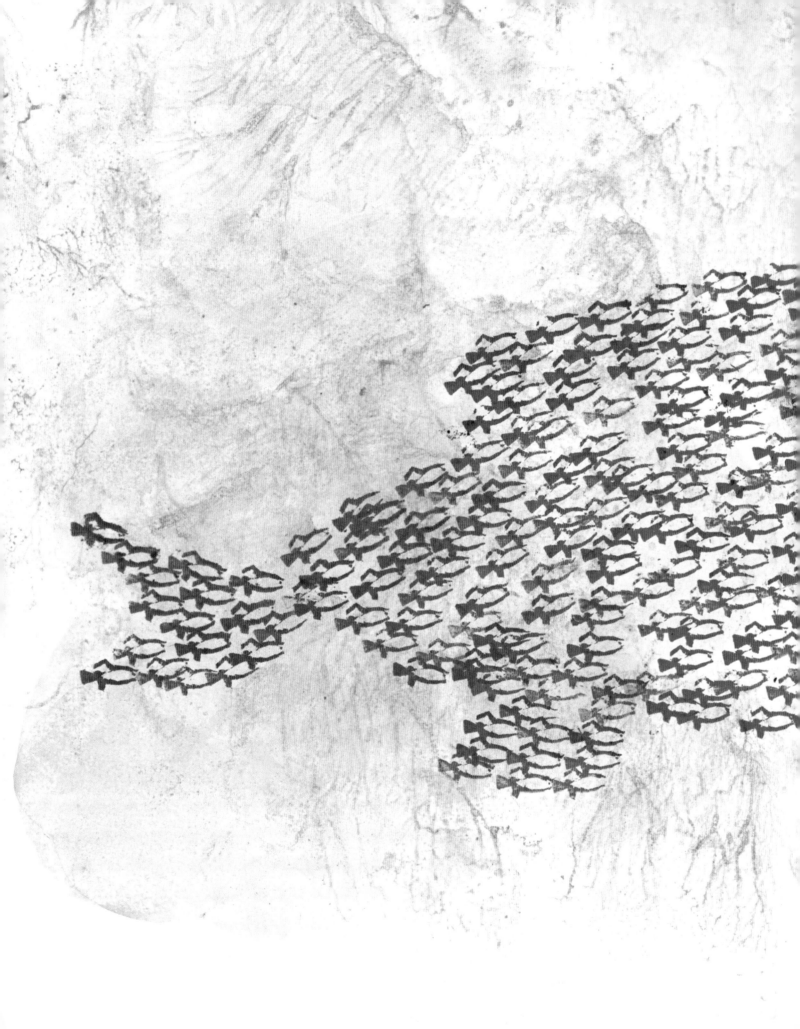

and when they had learned to swim like one giant fish, he said, "I'll be the eye."

And so they swam in the cool morning water and in the midday sun and

chased the big fish away.

THIS IS A BORZOI BOOK PUBLISHED BY ALFRED A. KNOPF

Copyright © 1963, copyright renewed 1991 by Leo Lionni
Tribute copyright © 2013 by Eric Carle

All rights reserved. Published in the United States by Alfred A. Knopf, an imprint of Random House
Children's Books, a division of Random House, Inc., New York. Originally published by Pantheon Books,
a division of Random House, Inc., New York, in 1963.

Knopf, Borzoi Books, and the colophon are registered trademarks of Random House, Inc.

Visit us on the Web! randomhouse.com/kids
Educators and librarians, for a variety of teaching tools, visit us at RHTeachersLibrarians.com

Library of Congress Cataloging-in-Publication Data is available upon request.

ISBN 978-0-385-75358-6 (trade) — ISBN 978-0-385-75366-1 (lib. bdg.)

MANUFACTURED IN CHINA
June 2013
10 9 8 7 6 5 4 3 2 1
First Anniversary Edition